Felix the Fast Tractor
and the Twirling Tractors

This Red Wellies book
belongs to

_____

_____

CATHERINE CANNON

for Peter and Emma
and everyone at Penrith Show
www.penrithshow.co.uk

Look out for further illustrated stories about Felix the Fast Tractor
by Catherine Cannon.

Visit www.felixthefasttractor.co.uk
for some fun colouring and games.

First published in Great Britain by Red Wellies Publishing in 2009.

ISBN 0-9547701-4-5
ISBN 978-0-9547701-4-3

Text and illustrations copyright © Catherine Cannon 2009.
The author/illustrator asserts the moral right to be identified as the author/illustrator of the work.

A CIP catalogue record for this title is available from the British Library.

First Edition

Designed by Dave Walters. Printed by Reeds Printers, Penrith.

Felix the Fast Tractor
and the Twirling Tractors

CATHERINE CANNON

Red Wellies Publishing

Illustrations by Ron Ablewhite

Felix the Fast Tractor lives on Ambers Farm
with Farmer Story, Mrs Story, their two children -
Max and Lucy - and the family dog, Ben.

Felix loves living on a farm - there is always plenty
to do and lots of people around. In fact, Felix couldn't
think of anywhere else that he would rather live.

Felix was helping Farmer Story
and Farmer Brougham (sounds like broom)
to get ready for the local farming show.
All day long he carried fences in his trailer
to make pens for the animals.

Felix had been working really hard,
but whenever he had a minute to spare he stopped
to watch the Twirling Tractors - Olly, Polly, Molly and Wally
practise their routine to perform at the show.

He had never seen tractors do anything so exciting.
Olly, Polly, Molly and Wally were the best!

Want to know more about animal pens?

A pen is an enclosure for holding livestock, often used to house animals such as sheep, cows and pigs at farming shows.

As Felix slept in his cosy barn
he dreamt of being a Twirling Tractor.
He pulled wheelies, and performed a perfect
figure of eight, just like
Olly, Polly, Molly and Wally.

If only dreams could come true!

7

The day of the show finally arrived
and everyone was very excited.

Thankfully, the sun was shining too.

As well as looking after Ben, Max was
looking after Farmer Brougham's dog, Beacon.
Both dogs were proving to be a bit of a handful!

At the show Max and Lucy couldn't wait
to visit the marquees, which were full of
wonderful things that people had made.

Beautiful gingerbread houses,
gorgeous, gooey buns and
fantastic birthday cakes
all looked delicious.

**Want to know more
about a marquee?**

A marquee is a large tent
often used at shows,
events and weddings.

Lucy had entered
a competition to
'MAKE AN ANIMAL
FROM FRUIT
AND VEGETABLES'
and she was delighted
to have won first prize
for her fruity bear.
Well done, Lucy!

But what was
even more
exciting for Lucy
was seeing
the lovely
Shetland ponies.

Unfortunately, Max hadn't
done so well in the
'CHILD WITH A SHEEPDOG'
competition because Ben and Beacon
wouldn't sit still long
enough to win a prize.
Poor Max!

Victor the Vet and Farmer Story
had an important job to do,
as they were judging the Swaledale sheep.
They carefully checked the animals,
looking at their colour
and woolly coats.

**Want to know more
about judging sheep?**

When checking sheep
the judge will look at the
colour, markings and
woolly coat of the animals.

The end of the show drew near
and Felix could hardly hide his excitement.
The Twirling Tractors were due to start
their performance in the main ring
and crowds of people were gathering
to watch them.

But Farmer Brougham
was looking far from happy.
In fact, he looked
very worried.

Wally, one of the
Twirling Tractors,
had a puncture.
They couldn't perform
their routine with
only three tractors.
Farmer Brougham wanted
Felix to be the fourth
Twirling Tractor!

Felix thought for a moment, then nodded slowly.

He could do this.

He was a fast, brave, clever tractor.

But he was also a teeny-weeny bit nervous!

Felix drove into the main ring and stood with Molly,
who gave him an encouraging wink.
Farmer Brougham stood with his microphone.

"Let's give a big warm welcome to
the Twirling Tractors, Olly, Polly, Molly,
and for one day only,
our very own FELIX!"

"Please DO NOT
try this at home!" added
Farmer Brougham.

The music began and the Twirling Tractors
drove in a circle around the ring,
gathering speed as they went.

Gradually, Felix began to relax as he followed
Olly, Polly and Molly into a figure of eight.

Felix was revving and gathering speed,
going round and round until he finally got
his balance on two wheels.
Well done, Felix!

To end the routine the Twirling Tractors
took it in turns to pull wheelies,
so they were just balancing on their back tyres.

The tractors were brilliant and the show
had been a great success!

As Felix returned from his twirling,
Farmer Brougham and the Story family
clapped and cheered.

They were all very proud of Felix -
he had certainly saved the day!

As everyone left the show that evening,
they were all still chatting about
Felix's fantastic twirling!

Why not make an animal
out of fruit and vegetables, just like Lucy?
Here are a few ideas to get you started.

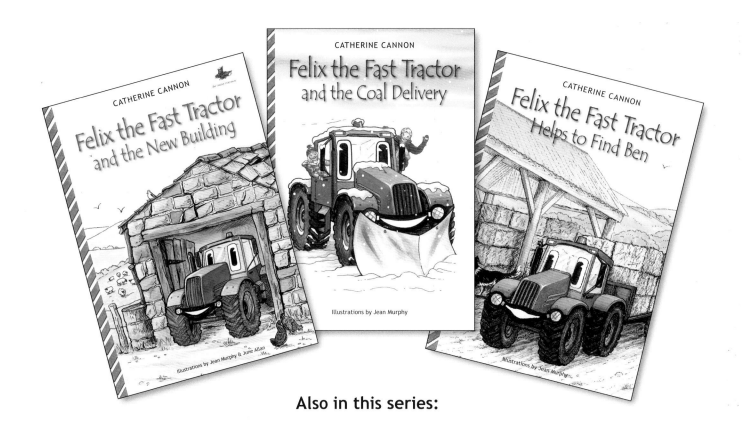

Also in this series:

Felix the Fast Tractor and the New Building

Follow Felix and his friends as they construct a new building on the farm - but what is it for? That's a secret!

Felix the Fast Tractor and the Coal Delivery

Felix helps Andrew the Coalman with a delivery of coal in snowy weather - but can they make it on time?

Felix the Fast Tractor Helps to Find Ben

Felix and his friends are harvesting when Ben the dog goes missing - where can he be?

Visit Felix and his friends at

www.felixthefasttractor.co.uk